HEIDI HECKELBECK

Lights! Camera! Awesome!

By Wanda Coven

Illustrated by Priscilla Burris

LITTLE SIMON

New York London Toronto Sydney New Delhi

LITTLE SIMON
An imprint of Simon & Schuster Children's Publishing Division
1230 Avenue of the Americas, New York, New York 10020
First Little Simon paperback edition December 2018
Copyright © 2018 by Simon & Schuster, Inc.
Also available in a Little Simon hardcover edition.
All rights reserved, including the right of reproduction in whole or in part in any form. LITTLE SIMON is a registered trademark of Simon & Schuster, Inc., and associated colophon is a trademark of Simon & Schuster, Inc. For information about special discounts for bulk purchases, please contact Simon & Schuster Special Sales at 1-866-506-1949 or business@simonandschuster.com. The Simon & Schuster Speakers Bureau can bring authors to your live event. For more information or to book an event contact the Simon & Schuster Speakers Bureau at 1-866-248-3049 or visit our website at www.simonspeakers.com.
Designed by Ciara Gay
Manufactured in the United States of America 1118 MTN
10 9 8 7 6 5 4 3 2 1
This book has been cataloged with the Library of Congress.
ISBN 978-1-5344-2648-1 (hc)
ISBN 978-1-5344-2647-4 (pbk)
ISBN 978-1-5344-2649-8 (eBook)

Chapter 1

HOW TO BE FAMOUS

"Roar!"

"ROAR!"

"ROARRR!"

Heidi Heckelbeck and her best friend Lucy Lancaster squealed and ran across the playground. They were playing Cheese Dinosaur Tag.

Stanley Stonewrecker dressed like a dinosaur. The rest of the class—or, at least, those who were playing—was the cheese. And, of course, in this game the dinosaur *loves* cheese and won't stop until he gets some.

"He'll never find us under here," Lucy whispered.

Heidi plunked onto the ground and accidentally bumped into a pair of pink polka-dot flats under the table. Heidi stared fearfully at the shoes because she knew exactly who they belonged to—Melanie Maplethorpe, her least favorite girl in the class.

Melanie peered under the table and glared at Heidi. "What do you think you're doing?" she cried, pushing the toe of her shoe into Heidi's side.

"Sorry," said Heidi. She dragged out the word like *saw-ree*.

Then Lucy noticed Melanie had a magazine in her hand.

"What are you reading?" asked Lucy, trying to change the mood under the table.

Melanie turned her new magazine around so Lucy and Heidi could see the cover.

"I'm reading *She-She* magazine," Melanie said, lightening up. "It's my absolute favorite." *She-She* magazine had all the latest tween fashions and celebrity gossip.

"This SPECIAL issue has advice on how to be FAMOUS," Melanie went on. "And if there's one thing I want to be, it's FAMOUS!"

Then Melanie slid underneath the table beside the girls.

"Do you want to hear some tips on how to be famous?" Melanie asked.

Heidi and Lucy looked at each other in surprise. Melanie rarely ever shared anything, except maybe insults.

"Okay, sure!" Lucy said.

Melanie smiled and opened up her magazine. "Okay. 'Tip number one,'" she began. "'When you're famous, you always have to dress like you're walking on a runway—that's because everyone wants to take your picture.'"

Melanie showed celebrities posing for pictures. Then she turned the page.

"'Tip number two: You'll want your fans to think you're normal,' so you have to shop for everyday things, like oranges."

Melanie showed a picture of a pretty girl in dark glasses picking an orange from an orange display.

"'Tip number three,'" Melanie said. "'You really have to like FANCY things.'

This one's super-easy for me because I LOVE fancy things. Like, one time I ate SUSHI. That's very fancy."

Heidi and Lucy nodded.

"Last but not least," Melanie went on, "'tip number four: You have to be okay with people being completely jealous of your perfect, amazing superstar life.'" Then she closed her magazine and sighed loudly. "And I'm totally fine with that."

Then, out of nowhere, Stanley's face appeared under the table.

"ROAR!!!"

The girls screamed. Heidi and Lucy crawled away as fast as they could and hid behind a tree. Heidi peeked out from behind the trunk.

Stanley waved over to Melanie. "Hi! Are you playing?" he asked her. Melanie just stuck her nose back in her magazine. "No, I am not. Because famous stars DO NOT ever play Cheese Dinosaur Tag."

Then Heidi turned to Lucy. "Wow, I'm sure glad I'M not famous," she said, "because I LOVE to play Cheese Dinosaur Tag!"

Chapter 2

THE HOST OF OUR SHOW!

After recess, Principal Pennypacker visited Heidi's classroom. "I have wonderful news!" he began, rubbing his hands together with excitement. "Brewster Elementary is going to have its very own school news show. And we need someone to host it."

Sha-zoom! Melanie's hand shot up like a space rocket launcher. The principal nodded toward her.

"Host?" she asked. "So I could be a host on TV?"

Principal Pennypacker chuckled. "Yes, Melanie—just like that. Only this show would not be a Hollywood production. It would be for our school community."

Then the principal held up a sheet of paper. "Here is the sign-up sheet. If you'd like to be considered as a host, you will need to sign up and make a sample video with the help of your parents. In the video you should tell us one thing about the school that you would like to talk about."

Melanie's hand shot up again.

"Yes, Melanie?"

She jumped out of her seat. "May I pass around the sign-up sheet and collect signatures?" she asked.

The principal walked over to Melanie's seat and placed the sign-up sheet on her desk. She instantly grabbed her pen and signed her name on the top line.

This was not surprising to Heidi. *Melanie had to be the first one to sign up, of course,* she thought.

"Once the videos are all in," the principal continued, "the class will watch them and vote on who should be our school news host."

Then the kids in the class all began to talk at once.

"I signed up!" Lucy told Bruce. "Did you?"

Bruce nodded. Then both of the friends hurried over to Heidi's desk. Heidi stared at the sign-up sheet uncertainly.

"Go ahead, Heidi! Sign up!" Lucy encouraged her. "We did!"

Heidi slowly unzipped her pencil case and pulled out a cinnamon roll–scented pencil.

Melanie stood next to Heidi's desk and tapped her foot impatiently.

"Why even bother signing up, Heidi?" Melanie asked. "You're not exactly the TV show host type. I mean, what if you make a MISTAKE and everyone LAUGHS at you?"

Heidi felt her cheeks grow warm. *That Smell-a-nie is NOT going to tell ME what to do,* she thought. Then Heidi pressed her pencil firmly on the line and signed her name.

Melanie humphed. "Well, you'll never beat me," she said, snatching the sign-up sheet back from Heidi. "I was born to be famous."

Heidi folded her arms. *Ugh,* she thought. *Melanie's right. She probably will beat me. And why did I sign up anyway? I hate being in the spotlight. Merg.*

Chapter 3

BLOOPERS

A few days later, Heidi told her family about the school news program and how—for some dumb reason—she had signed up to make a video.

"Don't worry," Henry said. "I know the perfect thing you can do for your video!"

He ran to the hall closet and put on his raincoat, rain hat, and boots. He set a table fan on the counter and switched it on full blast. Then he grabbed a large spoon and held it in front of his mouth.

"This is Henry Heckelbeck, coming to you LIVE from the middle of a Category 5 hurricane," he reported.

He tilted his head toward the fan, and his rain hat blew off. Then he pretended to brace himself against a gale-force wind.

"Do not go outside!" he warned. "This storm is a DOOZY!"

Everyone laughed—even Heidi, who didn't usually find Henry particularly funny. Henry bowed and sat back down on his chair.

"So, what are you going to make your video about?" Dad asked.

Heidi twirled her spaghetti with her fork. "I have no idea," she said at first. "But maybe I can talk about how our school library could use some new books."

Mom and Dad looked at each other and smiled.

"Now, *that's* a stellar idea!" praised Dad.

Mom nodded. "You can use the bookcase in the den as a backdrop."

Heidi began to get excited about making her video. Since her friends had already finished their videos, she invited Lucy and Bruce over the next day to help. They made cue cards and dragged a comfy chair in front of the bookcase.

"Oh, can I be the director?" Lucy asked. She pointed to the chair. "Sit here and pretend you are reading a book. Then talk about how much you like to read."

Heidi plopped onto the chair with a book.

Bruce set up the camera to make sure everything was perfect. "Ready?" he said.

Heidi nodded and opened the book.

"Action!" cried Lucy.

Heidi looked up from her book. "Oh, hi, I'm Heydee—wait, I mean, hey, I'm Hi-dee-aye-yiy-yiy. Oopsie—I messed up."

Lucy waved her hand in front of the camera. "CUT!" she said.

Heidi took a sip of water. "Okay, I'm really ready this time," she said.

Bruce began to film. "Oh no! CUT!" he said. "You got water all over yourself."

Lucy grabbed a tissue and handed it to Heidi. Heidi wiped her face and dabbed her shirt. They started again.

"Action!" Lucy cried.

Heidi looked up from her book. "Hi, I'm Heidi, and . . . and . . . and I forgot my next line."

Lucy held up a cue card. "And you LOVE books!" she whispered.

Heidi bounced in her chair. "Oh yeah!" she said. "Now I'm seriously ready."

Lucy clapped her hands in front of the camera. "And ACTION!" she cried again.

Heidi looked up from her book.

"Hi, I'm Heidi, and . . . OUCH!" A paper airplane had hit her in the side of the head. She whirled around and caught Henry making goofy faces at the camera from behind the chair.

Heidi held up her book as if she were going to bonk her little brother.

"Beat it!" she shouted.

Henry screamed and ran. And after that, Heidi tried and tried and tried again, but she couldn't get the video right. Soon Lucy and Bruce had to go home. They hadn't even gotten *one* good take—just a bunch of bloopers! Mom grabbed the camera.

"I'll take it from here," she said.

As the night went on, Mom and Heidi worked on the video for two more hours. Finally they made a good version, except for one teensy thing. . . . Heidi was holding her book upside down at the end.

"I'm sure no one will notice," Mom said with a yawn.

Heidi folded her arms. "Mom, how can you NOT notice? The picture on the cover is UPSIDE DOWN."

Heidi really wanted to fix her video, but it was already time for bed. Even Mom was falling asleep.

Chapter 4

LIGHTS! CAMERA! AWESOME!

Heidi brushed her teeth and looked in the bathroom mirror. She held her toothbrush up like a microphone.

"Hello, I'm Heidi Heckelbeck, and I'm reporting today from my house, speaking with a girl who is a real professional video messer-upper."

43

Then Heidi saw dried toothpaste in the corners of her mouth.

"Merg! There is NO WAY I'm going to let my whole class see me mess up in that video," she announced. "Melanie would never stop making fun of me."

Heidi marched into her room and grabbed her *Book of Spells* from under the bed.

There has to be a spell in here somewhere that can help me, she thought. Heidi flipped through the pages and found a spell to make you glamorous and a spell to make you a good writer. Then she landed on the perfect spell called Lights! Camera! Awesome!

Lights! Camera! Awesome!

Do you flub things when you try to make a video? Maybe you get tongue-tied and forget your lines. Do you ever fumble with your props? Or perhaps a video-gremlin tries to distract you? If you'd like to make a flawless video, then this is the spell for you!

Ingredients:
1 pair of movie-star sunglasses
1 cup of milk
2 tablespoons of spicy hot sauce
A dash of glitter stars

Mix the ingredients together in a bowl. Hold your Witches of Westwick medallion in one hand, and hold the other hand over the mix. Chant the following spell:

LIGHTS ARE ON!

HOLDING STEADY!

MAKE MY VIDEO CAMERA-READY!

Heidi gathered the ingredients, dumped them into a bowl, and stirred everything together. Holding her medallion in one hand, she put her other one over the mix. Then she chanted the spell.

No sooner had she finished than a feeling of confidence swept over

her. Heidi ran down-
stairs and asked her
mother if she could
try to make one more
video.

Mom sighed, but
Heidi pleaded until
her mother couldn't say no.

"Okay, okay," Mom agreed. "But
this is the very last time!"
And it *was* the very
last time, because Heidi
knew this take would
be magical!

THE STARS ARE OUT TONIGHT!

Finally it was presentation day! Heidi filed into the auditorium with her classmates. She couldn't wait to see her video on the big screen. *Being a star might not be so bad after all,* she thought. Then Principal Pennypacker announced the order of the videos.

Lucy was up first. The lights dimmed. Everyone watched her jog across the screen in her soccer outfit.

"Hi, my name is Lucy Lancaster, and I'm, um, here to talk about, um, um, um Brewster sports!" she said, picking up her ball and facing the camera. "Here at Brewster, we, um, like to play all kinds of, um, sports." Her video showed kids playing four-square, swinging on the monkey bars, and playing soccer and basketball.

The theme song from *Rocky* played in the background.

Heidi squeezed Lucy's arm when it was over. "That was really good!" she whispered—even though she thought Lucy said "um" a lot.

After a few other videos it was Bruce's turn. He filmed his video in the science lab and wore his lab coat and safety glasses.

"Hi there, I'm Bruce Bickerson, and today I am going to teach you how to make homemade root beer."

Bruce began to pour water into a large pot. Some of the water spilled all over. Then he tore open the packet of root beer flavoring and dropped the packet on the floor. When the root beer was finally finished, he poured it into the bottles, and it dripped down the sides. His video was messy, but it was also a lot of fun.

Heidi turned to Bruce, who was sitting on the other side of her.

"That was really cool," she said—even though Bruce had acted a little nervous and clumsy.

Stanley was up next. He sat at a lunch table and talked about cafeteria food in his video. He ate both breakfast and lunch every day for a week, but on film, it looked like he was just eating one meal after another.

"Super-awesome pancakes!" *Munch! Munch! Munch!* "Mysterious meatballs!" *Chomp! Chomp! Chomp!* "Crunchy corn-dogs!" *Munch! Crunch! Munch!*

Stanley talked with his mouth full and spewed food everywhere. The class laughed and whistled because Stanley looked like a P-I-G.

Then Melanie made her splash on the big screen. She talked about the lights at school.

"Fluorescent lights make people look terrible," Melanie began. "So I suggest we remove Brewster's harsh white lights and replace them with softer ones. This will make students more alert, and best of all—it'll make them look FABULOUS!"

Then Melanie showed an example of good lighting. "See how the lights  in my bedroom make my hair look shiny and my skin look flawless?"

She posed this way and that.

"Let's rethink the lights at school so everyone could look as good as me! TTFN!" And Melanie waved good-bye.

The class erupted into claps and cheers. Even Heidi thought Melanie's video was amazing. She was easy to understand and totally charming—though she talked about herself a little too much, but that was just Melanie being Melanie.

Then it was time. Heidi grabbed her armrests, sat up, and stared at the screen. Her video was about to start.

Now it's MY turn! she said to herself.

Chapter 6

A REAL SUPERSTAR

The students fell silent as Heidi's charmed video began.

"Oh, hi there, I'm Heidi," she said in her casual, under-the-spell voice. "And you caught me in the middle of a great book." She set the book on the table next to her.

"I love to read books everywhere!" she went on. "Like in this comfy chair, or under my covers with a flashlight, or even way up in a tree fort." Heidi's video showed clips of all the places she liked to read. "The only problem is, I've read everything in the school library. But I have an idea for our library to get new books."

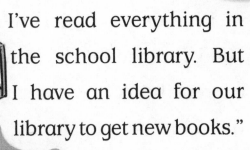

Heidi paused and looked at the camera for a moment. "If every student gave the library one book on their birthday, then think how many new books our library would have by the end of the year. So join me in helping make our school a better place, where we can all read happily ever after."

As the screen went dark, everyone cheered for Heidi—even Melanie.
Then the students voted for the video
they liked best.

On the way back to the classroom,
Heidi's classmates swarmed around
her.

"Your video was just the BEST!" said Bruce.

"Oh, I loved your idea for the school library!" Lucy said.

"Wow! Your video should totally WIN!" added Stanley.

Heidi just couldn't believe it. And the weirdest thing of all was that nobody was congratulating Melanie—even though her video had been amazing too.

Principal Pennypacker returned to the classroom to announce the winner. He walked to the front of the room and cleared his throat.

"Your videos were wonderful," he said. "And believe it or not, we have a *tie*."

The students gasped. Principal Pennypacker held up his hands to quiet the class.

"This means Brewster's school news program will have cohosts! Now let's congratulate our very own Heidi Heckelbeck and Melanie Maplethorpe!"

The whole class cheered. Heidi's mouth hung open in disbelief.

Wow, she thought. *I'm a real SUPERSTAR!*

THE IT GIRL

The next day Heidi got off the school bus and found a big surprise. Her adoring fans were all waiting for her.

"There she is!" Laurel Lambert shouted.

"I saw her FIRST!" Natalie Newman cried.

Everyone ran to greet her. Some kids even asked her for an autograph. Heidi didn't mind. She signed their notebooks and binders. *This is so cool,* she thought. Then Heidi noticed everyone in her class was wearing headbands just like hers—even the boys.

Lucy pulled Heidi by the arm. "Follow me!" she said.

Lucy led Heidi inside the school and down a red carpet that went all the way to Heidi's desk. It was not a real carpet, it was a pathway of red construction paper taped to the floor to make it look like a red carpet.

Cameras flashed as Heidi walked along.

"Let's get a picture of our cohosts together!" said Mrs. Welli, the teacher, as Heidi entered the classroom. Melanie posed next to Heidi. She put one hand on her hip and the other one in the air.

Click! Click! Click!

Finally Heidi sat down at her desk, which was covered with candy, flowers, and a cute teddy bear holding a microphone. The class thought up names for the new show. Mrs. Welli wrote them on the board.

The Brewster News Hour

The Brewster Buzz

The Brewster Bulletin

The Brewster Files

Then they voted.

"And the winning name is . . . *The Brewster Buzz!*" Mrs. Welli announced, which was, of course, Heidi's idea.

Heidi got the same star treatment in the library, too. Mrs. Williams, the librarian, hung a banner in Heidi's honor. It said HOORAY FOR HEIDI! THE STAR OF THE LIBRARY!

"Our library has already received five new books!" Mrs. Williams said. "All thanks to your great idea, Heidi."

HOORAY FOR HEIDI!
THE STAR OF THE LIBRARY!

Every class was the same. In science the class got to drink Bruce's homemade root beer in honor of Heidi.

In art Mr. Doodlebee had everyone make a mural about Heidi's video.

And at lunch everyone wanted to sit next to the class star. *So this is what it feels like to be FAMOUS,* Heidi thought.

After lunch Heidi needed to be
alone to learn her lines—much to
the disappointment of her fans. She
heard people talking about her as she
walked away.

"Isn't Heidi awesome?"

"She's the coolest!"

"We're so lucky we go to the SAME school as HEIDI HECKELBECK!"

Heidi had a swing in her step. *Swag on!* she said to herself.

Chapter 8

FALLiNG STAR

Heidi and Melanie met in the auditorium to record the first episode of *The Brewster Buzz*. A backdrop had been set up on the stage, which had special lights and a microphone overhead. Bruce had been chosen to run the video camera.

Principal Pennypacker clapped his hands. "Okay, let's get started," he said. "Heidi, please begin with this week's cafeteria menu."

Heidi walked in front of the backdrop. Bruce held up his video camera and made a few adjustments.

"Ready?" he asked.

Heidi nodded, but she didn't feel ready at all. Her mouth was so dry that it felt like it was filled with cotton.

The principal lifted the bar on his clapboard. "School menu, take one!" he said. "And ACTION!" He snapped the clapboard.

Heidi looked uncertainly at the camera. "Hi . . . I'm Heidi . . . and this is the cafeteria menu . . . for Monday." Heidi sounded like a scared robot, but she kept going.

"Today we'll be having dot hogs. I mean, not dogs! Oops, make that hot dots!"

The principal waved his hands. "Cut! Cut! Cut!" he said. "Melanie, would you please get our star some water?"

Melanie ran and got Heidi a bottle of water. Heidi unscrewed the cap top and pressed the cool drink against her lips.

The water dribbled down the front of her shirt. She brushed herself off and set the bottle on a table, but it tipped over and spilled right onto Melanie's script.

Melanie squealed. "Be careful!"

Heidi wiped the water off the script. *Uh-oh,* she thought. *I think my spell must have worn off.*

"Take two!" Principal Pennypacker called out. "And ACTION."

Heidi jumped to attention. "Hi, I'm Heidi, and this is the cough-a-teria. I mean cer-for-tar-ia. Oh no! Coffee-teer-ee-a."

"Cut!" cried Principal Pennypacker. "Heidi, maybe you need a short break. Melanie can do her part, and then we'll get back to you."

Heidi nodded in relief.

Melanie pranced in front of the backdrop and pulled out a compact mirror.

"This is great lighting, Principal Pennypacker," she said. "It gives my skin just the right glow."

"Well, I'm very glad you approve, Melanie," Principal Pennypacker said. "Are you ready?"

Melanie nodded.

The principal stepped back. "ACTION!"

Melanie smiled at the camera as if it were her best friend.

"Hello, everyone," she said. "I'm Melanie Maplethorpe for *The Brewster Buzz*. Next week is our annual Fund Run—and you know what that means?!"

Melanie winked.

"It means next week is Spirit Week! And we'll have Crazy Hair Day on Monday! Silly Hat Tuesday! Wacky Tacky Wednesday! Superhero Thursday! And Friday we'll RUN to raise money for our school! Don't forget your pledge forms and TTFN!"

"And . . . cut!" cheered Principal Pennypacker. "*Well done*, Melanie! Not a single mistake."

Melanie curtsied. "I just LOVE the camera," she said dreamily. "And the camera loves ME."

Heidi agreed. Melanie was a true natural. Now Heidi felt like a big fat fraud. She had looked so good in her video, but she knew that wasn't really her—it had been the spell.

I'm not an awesome celebrity star after all, she owned up to herself. *I'm more like a falling star.*

Chapter 9

BEHIND THE SCENES

Heidi crept off the stage while Principal Pennypacker and Melanie were talking. She hid behind one of the sets—a cluster of trees. *Nobody will notice me back here,* she thought. But Heidi was wrong.

Someone did notice.

"Heidi?"

It was Melanie. Heidi wanted to run, but she was trapped between the set and the wall. She braced herself for Melanie's wisecracks.

"Hey, Heidi," Melanie said, but her voice didn't sound mean this time. It actually sounded nice. "I know exactly how it feels to be shy in front of a camera."

Heidi looked up. "You DO?"

Melanie nodded. "I used to feel that way too," she said. "But my acting coach taught me some tricks to keep the jitters away. Want to hear some?"

Heidi felt her shoulders relax. "Sure, I'd really like that."

Melanie smiled. "First, you have to stand up straight with your head up and your shoulders back."

Heidi stood up tall.

"Now take a deep breath in slowly through your nose and then exhale slowly through your mouth," Melanie continued. "This will relax you."

Heidi breathed slowly in and out.

"That's good," praised Melanie. "Now, believe it or not, tongue twisters will help you speak more clearly. Try this one: Do drop in at the Dew Drop Inn."

Heidi repeated the phrase.

"Perfect!" Melanie said. "Now try another one: Silly Sara sold soggy sushi by the seashore."

Heidi giggled as she repeated the phrase.

"Now—and this is really, REALLY important—pretend the camera is your very best friend, and you'll be able to talk naturally," Melanie said. "Got it?"

Heidi nodded, and the girls walked back to the set.

"Ready?" Principal Pennypacker asked. Heidi got in position.

"Just have FUN with it," Melanie said.

This time Heidi pretended that the camera was her best friend Lucy.

"Hey, I'm Heidi, and I'm here to tell you about Monday's school cafeteria

lunch. We're going to have hot dogs—
one of my personal favorites—baked
barbecue potato chips, and strawberry
yogurt for dessert. Yum!"

Heidi got through the whole thing
without one mistake. She wasn't as
smooth as Melanie, but she did okay.

"Way to go!" Melanie cheered.

Heidi smiled. Then she walked over to the principal and tapped him on the arm.

"What is it, Heidi?"

Heidi took a deep breath. "I think Melanie should host the show all by herself," she said. "She's the right one for the job—not both of us."

Principal Pennypacker gave a quick wink. "Okay, Heidi. I understand. It's possible that not every-one is meant to be Lights! Camera! Awesome!"

Heidi's eyes grew round.

That's weird, she thought. *He just said the exact name of the spell!*

Chapter 10

FIFTEEN MINUTES OF FAME

Heidi sat between Lucy and Bruce in the auditorium. *The Brewster Buzz* was about to air for the first time. The whole school was there.

The show opened with clips of Melanie reporting from the library, on the playground, and in the cafeteria.

The crowd clapped and cheered. Then Melanie reported on the upcoming Fund Run, along with the school play, which was *The Sound of Music*, and an art exhibit that Mr. Doodlebee had set up in the learning center.

"And NOW," Melanie said excitedly, "here to present the instructions for the game that's sweeping the Brewster playground is our on-the-spot reporter, Heidi Heckelbeck!"

The crowd whistled and hollered as the screen went black.

The new scene zoomed in on Heidi. She held a microphone and stood on the playground beside Stanley.

"Hi, everyone," Heidi said. Then she jerked her thumb at Stanley. "THIS is a dinosaur."

Stanley raised his hands like they were the claws of a T. rex. "ROAR!" he snarled, and the audience shrieked with laughter.

"And OVER HERE," Heidi said, pointing to a group of students, including Lucy and Bruce, "we have some CHEESE."

The kids who were the cheese all waved to the camera.

"Now, the object of the game is for the dinosaur to grab some cheese. Does anyone know WHY?"

Heidi held the microphone out to the playground and everyone shouted, "Because dinosaurs LOVE cheese!"

Then Heidi turned back to Stanley and cried, "Go get 'em, dinosaur!"

Then the kids who were cheese screamed and scattered on the playground. Stanley chased after them.

"And that's how you play Cheese Dinosaur Tag," Heidi said, pumping her eyebrows. Then she turned her head to one side.

Someone off camera said, "I spy

some SWISS CHEESE! Swiss is my FAVORITE kind! ROAR!"

Heidi looked at the camera, screamed, and ran across the play-ground. Stanley the Dinosaur chased after her as the video faded to black.

Everyone in the auditorium howled with laughter.

The Brewster Buzz was a big hit. Melanie may have been the true *star* of the show, but Heidi had become a Cheese Dinosaur Tag *legend*.

ROAR!

Check out the next book starring **HEiDi HECKELBECK**

Splurt!

Splurt!

Splurt!

Heidi Heckelbeck squeezed a glob of craft glue into a mixing bowl. Then she squirted some shaving cream on top. Next she sprinkled some contact lens solution into the mix. Finally, she added the special liquid activator.

An excerpt from *Heidi Heckelbeck Lends a Helping Hand*

Heidi swirled the ingredients together like a magic potion—only this wasn't actually a potion.

Today, in her art class, she was making a huge bowl of *slime*. Fluffy slime, to be exact.

She stirred until the slime pulled away from the bowl and became a big fluff-o-luscious *blob*. Then she poked the slime with all ten fingers.

"It's so squishable!" she said, squeezing it with her hands.

Lucy Lancaster, who was sitting next to Heidi, peeked into Heidi's bowl.

An excerpt from *Heidi Heckelbeck Lends a Helping Hand*

"Oooh!" she exclaimed, stirring her own mix faster to catch up. "Your slime looks so marshmallowy!"

Heidi grabbed her slime and kneaded it like bread dough. The slime spoke a language all its own: *Skloop! Sklorp! Skleep!*

"Time to add some color!" Heidi announced. She plopped the slime back into the bowl and opened a package of neon-green powdered food coloring. She dumped the whole package of dye into the bowl. Then she slapped the slime with her hand. *POOF!*

An excerpt from *Heidi Heckelbeck Lends a Helping Hand*